Bob Saves the Porcupines

adapted by
Diane Redmond

based on the teleplay by
Chris Trengrove

SCHOLASTIC INC.
New York Toronto London Auckland Sydney
Mexico City New Delhi Hong Kong Buenos Aires

Based upon the television series *Bob the Builder*™ created by HIT Entertainment PLC
and Keith Chapman, with thanks to HOT Animation, as seen on Nick Jr.®

ISBN 0-439-40573-4

12 11 10 9 8 7 6 5 4 3 2 1   2 3 4 5 6 7/0

Printed in the U.S.A.

First Scholastic printing, December 2002

One day Spud and Travis were playing in the fields when Travis spotted something interesting.

"Hey, Spud," Travis called. "Look what I found—a family of upside-down hairbrushes!"

"They're not hairbrushes—they're porcupines!" said Spud, laughing.

Meanwhile, back at Farmer Pickles's house, Bob and the team were fixing a road.

Muck was backing up noisily.

"Left a bit . . . right a bit!" yelled Bob.

With a loud squeak Muck stopped and poured gravel onto the road.

"Great job!" shouted Bob. "Now, Scoop, I need you to spread the gravel evenly to give the road a nice new surface."

With a mighty heave Scoop pushed the pile of gravel across the road.

"Roley, it's all yours!" called Bob. "Roll the surface nice and flat!"

Roley was just about to roll over the stones when suddenly Bob spotted the porcupines.

"Roley, look out!" Bob shouted. "There are porcupines on the road!"

Roley screeched to a halt.

"Porcupines? Where?" Roley asked.
"Right under your nose!" cried Scoop.

"Now what are we going to do?" asked Bob. "We can't open this road to traffic. These porcupines won't be safe."

"How can we help the porcupines cross the road safely?" Scoop asked.

"Maybe we can build a bridge so they can go *over* the road?" Muck suggested.

"Don't think *over!*" cried Scoop. "Think *under!*"

"That's a great idea, Scoop!" Bob exclaimed. "We'll build a tunnel so that the porcupines can go *under* the road. Let's get to work."

"What are the porcupines going to do while we work?" asked Muck.

"Good point," said Bob. "Take them to the yard for now, Muck. And when you come back, bring some pipes with you, please."

Back at the office, Wendy's phone rang.

"Bob's building yard," she answered.

"Hello, Wendy," said Bob. "I'm just calling to tell you that Muck's coming over to the yard—with a family of porcupines!"

"Okay, Bob," said Wendy.

Muck chugged along the road, scoop raised high so that the porcupines could have a good look around.

"Hi, Muck," called Dizzy when Muck arrived back at the yard. "What are you doing back so early?"

"I'm on a porcupine rescue," Muck replied, proudly lowering them to the ground.

"Aaagh!" cried Lofty. "Mice with spikes!" He was scared.

"No, silly!" said Wendy, laughing as she came outside. "They're not mice—they're porcupines!"

Then she set a bowl of water on the ground for the porcupines to drink.

"Now, Muck, you better get going. Bob said he needed those pipes right away!"

Back at the road, Bob was deciding where to put the tunnel.

"You can start digging where my tape measure ends," he told Scoop.

"How are we going to get the porcupines back here?" asked Roley.

"I spoke to Wendy," Bob replied, smiling. "She's got a plan."

"It's time for you to go home, little ones!" said Wendy to the porcupines.

"Who's going to get them there?" asked Lofty, puzzled.

"*You're* going to take them," Wendy announced.

"Me?!" said Lofty with a gulp.

Wendy smiled and carefully loaded the porcupines into a basket, which she hung from Lofty's hook.

Lofty rode slowly through town with the basket. After a little while, he was so happy to be helping that he forgot to be scared of the porcupines at all.

Back at the road, Lofty carefully lowered the basket of porcupines. "I hope the porcupines like what we've done for them," said Scoop. "Now they will always be able to cross the road safely," said Bob. "Bye, porcupines!" shouted the machines as the porcupines scurried into the tunnel. "Good luck!"

"Look at that," said Bob. "My very first porcupine tunnel!"